Call From The Darkness

A COLLECTION OF DARK POETRY

LISA MICHELLE GORDIER

Call From The Darkness

A COLLECTION OF DARK POETRY

ReadersMagnet, LLC

Call From The Darkness: A Collection of Dark Poetry
Copyright © 2022 by Lisa Michelle Gordier

Published in the United States of America
ISBN Paperback: 978-1-956780-25-3
ISBN eBook: 978-1-956780-24-6

All rights reserved. No part of this publication may be reproduced, stored in a retrieval system or transmitted in any way by any means, electronic, mechanical, photocopy, recording or otherwise without the prior permission of the author except as provided by USA copyright law.

The opinions expressed by the author are not necessarily those of ReadersMagnet, LLC.

ReadersMagnet, LLC
10620 Treena Street, Suite 230 | San Diego, California, 92131 USA
1.619.354.2643 | www.readersmagnet.com

Book design copyright © 2022 by ReadersMagnet, LLC. All rights reserved.
Cover design by Ericka Obando
Interior design by Mary Mae Romero

Emptiness & Loneliness Calls

From where I stand,
Chill winds blow
through my soul.
And I stand,
Lost and alone.

Where emptiness follows,
And loneliness calls.

The only sound
is the wind.
Howling through,
Caverns wide,
Surrounding me.

Where emptiness follows,
And loneliness calls.

Nothing warms my soul.
Despair howls at my heels,
Like wolves at the door.
Yet when I turn,
There's nothing to mourn.

Where emptiness follows,
And loneliness calls.

To pits,
I am thrown.
To clouds,
I am raised.
I find nothing to praise.

Where emptiness follows,
And loneliness calls.

I search the depths
of my soul.
I seek the fringes,
of my thoughts.
I find and see nothing.

Where emptiness follows,
And loneliness calls.

Where do I run?
Where do I hide?
Where do I find,
Sounds of laughter
in this place?

Where emptiness follows,
And loneliness calls.

Tired

I am tired and have grown old.
My world is not what it once was.

I have come to the end of my road.
There is nowhere left to turn.

I cannot go forward; Death blocks my way.
I cannot go back; the past is gone forever.

I cannot go to either side
Other's lives were never mine to claim.

A Cry from Desolate Heart

I sit silent and alone
Pondering the world upon my throne
In darkness where shadows roam.

I listen to the silence of my heart
My soul longing for a new start
In the darkness of a shadow's heart.

Here I sit and here I stay
Here upon my throne where shadows play
In the darkness where devils play.

Death lurks beside me leaving me alone
Pondering what was once upon my throne
In the darkness where shadows roam.

Gone to the Darkness

I'm tired of light,
I'm tired of right.

I'm tired of morals,
I'm tired of purity.

Evil thoughts and vile deeds,
Lurk beyond the darkness.

Brewed in boredom,
Brewed in wretched hate so foul.

Here lurks madness.
Here lurks the pit of despair.

Here is where,
My soul ends in fear.

The light I have held,
Shrinks in haste.

Leaving darkness,
In its place.

Vile deeds of death,
Lurks through my mind.

Lucid darkness,
Hides my soul.

Where have I gone?
Where have I been?

Nowhere in truth,
For I have found;

I am tired of light,
I am tired of life.

I am tired of going,
Where God is bound.

Losing Heart

Where darkness rules and destruction falls,
Where shadows turn and sorrows boil,
Where madness flies and magic plays.

I am losing my heart.

My soul now builds its home here,
My mind now dwells in shadows,
And my heart plays with madness.

Once I stood firm in the light.

Away from the world's darkness and destruction
Away from shadows and sorrows of night
Away from the madness and magic of hell.

Now I stand surrounded by shadows.

With the destruction of my soul to come
With the sorrow of my mind to drown in
And the magic of my heart to become lost to.

Thus nothing remains.

No Tears

Though no tears
Fall from my eyes.
My heart and soul
Cry out in anguish.

My soul is twisted
And torn from its place.
My heart screams
And is rent asunder.

Tormented and lost
I wander alone.
I have fallen
And been ground
To dust and ashes.

Endlessly my soul
Cries out in anguish.

Yet no tears fall
from my Burning eyes.

Though I wallow
In a river of sorrow.
It seems no tears
Shall ever Grace my cheeks.

I am tormented
With the need
To end it all
Yet still, I go on,
Endlessly, wandering alone.

I am alone
In desolate emptiness.
Alone in darkness,
Alone in sorrow.

My heart and soul
Cry out in anguish.
And still no tears
Fall from my eyes.

The Price of Anger

In brief instance of pain
Lost in words
Forgetting the nature of love
Forgetting why they came

Anger was carelessly thrown
Tossed to and fro
Losing control of their hate
Bringing home their fate

Reason was lost
And love forgotten
Within the storm
Raging clouds grew

But then a child cried
Somehow they heard
Amidst the thunder
A silence grew

The silence
Seemed to say it all
Still, they could not speak
Could do nothing but weep

For the anger still held them
The words lay between them
The silence engulfed them
And love grew further away

No Better Than Before

Am I no better than before?

My soul eclipses my desire.
Rivers of tragedy shadow my love.
Wings of despair bind my heart

Now I experience dying seas
All plague my destiny.
Yet nothing stands in my way.

I look towards the horizon with hope.
Hope for the future
Things dreamed yet not seen.

Yet sadness stalks me.
Waves of horror threaten peace.
The world trudges onward without me.

My soul sinks into dying seas
And I am no better than before.

Can't Go Anywhere

I'm connected to a cord
Limited to where I can go.
Electricity runs through me
Trying to take away the pain.

A neuro-stimulator, they call it.
Surgically placed in my back.
Wires running up and down
Along with a battery making sure it runs.

Only one small problem with all of this,
Every few days the battery runs down.
Then back to the charger I must go.
Recharge that battery before it fails.
So less pain I will feel.

Now I'm back to that cord.
Back to laying on the couch,
Waiting for the battery to charge.
Connected to that darn cord,
Limited to where I can go.

Feathers & Chains

I am the wind caressed by feathers.
Feathers of my dearest Eagle's heart.
Yet storms have come and cast me down.
Chaining the soul of Heaven's Wind.

As the wind, I rage and howl in fury.
Lightning strikes, chains rattle in protest.
The eagle shall not fly far in such a storm.
Already feathers are floating down.

Chains are cast higher to hit the wretched bird.
How dare he chain my soul to the ground!
Surely the forming tornado will catch him.
There, I see more feathers flying past.

If I could just hit him one more time.
With chains, lightning and wind.
Come down, you foul bird, with the key!
Loose these chains so I may fly!

The winds I've called continue to churn.
Yet the Eagle seems to have gone.
Left me here in this storm in chains.
No more feathers to caress my soul.

The Eagle is gone forever.
Leaving feathers mingled with chains.
I hold out hope someone holds a key to free me.
For the wind should never be still.

The Last Curse

Dredging memories
Stark contrasts
What she used to be

Long ago in her element
Wearing African garb
In Orleans French Quarter

Brewing potions and spells
Throwing Hexes and curses
Never far, needed ingredients

Now are her darkest days
Lit only by fireflies
The companions of her grave

They know her secret
She would never seek solace
The last curse thrown

These Wretched Souls

Before me, on bloodied ground,
Lay countless wretched souls,
Mangled, in sweet despair.
Tears of sweet suffering,
Streak hollowed cheeks.

Baying of wolves come nearer,
Claws of winged beasts,
Already mark these souls.
Soon others will feast.
These poor souls cannot hide.

There was a time,
I might have cared.
No longer.

I long to be a winged beast,
Searching for its next victim.
I long to be the wolf,
Hunting in a pack with scent of prey.
Both, with wind beneath them, wild and free.

No Hope, All Fright

To end with no hope, all with fright
As Satan's demons call to our darker sides
We wallow in fear, loathing to his delight.

To end with no hope, all with fright.
God hears our cries, gives us light
As Satan's demons call to our darker sides
To end with no hope, all with fright.

Ship's Curse

Under the fierce gaze of a burning sun,
The voyage could hardly said be done.

Crew's expressions were grim,
A hard battle yet to begin.

The ship had been becalmed,
Wind stirred no sail upon yardarm.

Stores were dwindling rapidly,
Captain's voice grew gravelly.

Ships were meant to wander oceans blue,
Not sit idly waiting for their doom.

Precious little crew could do,
But wait for seas a new wind to brew.

Noble vessel waited with her crew,
How long, no one really knew.

She and they still wait,
In becalmed state.

Wishing for a simple breeze,
A breath of wind to set them free.

Depression for a Time

Black thoughts rush in
On dark trembling wings
Depression the mood for the day
Dark clouds, not sunshine weigh upon me

Light rushes from my path
Leering shadows come in its wake
Beasts of fear are lurking
Where once laughter played

Sorrows for time, love, family lost
Nothing will be as it once was
I know it's how life is to be
But today is a sad, terror-filled day

Shadows haunt the corner of my vision
Creatures of death plague my mind
Those dark trembling wings
Seems to forever surround me

The Final Darkness

Somewhere in darkness
Shadows creep
In dark corners
Nightmares haunt
My waking hours

Somewhere in darkness
My heart dwells
Dirt upon me
Six feet down
My feet stand firm

Somewhere in darkness
I'm laid to rest
Eyes weary
No more dreams
Lid closed

Knife Cries Guilty

A Knife in hand
Edge honed to perfection
Waiting to bite the hand it feeds

Thin slice of flesh

Life bleeds from fingertips
Dark red passage through veins
Pouring its story upon the floor

Thin slice of flesh

Time slowly passes
Red fountain appears
Pooling around its victim

Thin slice of flesh

The knife cries guilty
Still greedily hungering
For one more

Thin slice of flesh

When the Beast is Free

Roused from the darkness of my soul
The monster within chases me round.
With doors all open I cannot hide.
Nothing but bleak sadness surrounds me.

Where has my strong light retreated to?
I miss its warm glow upon my face.
With it the smell of apple blossoms
Which have now turned sour and decrepit.

Where has my strong light retreated to?
I miss its warm glow upon my face.
With it the smell of apple blossoms
Which have now turned sour and decrepit.

So darkness reigns and beast now runs free.

Depths of My Soul

Living
Inside breaking
Sanity of mind with
Astounding clarity

Making
Icicles of
Cheese and
Having
Eloquent cats
Languish
Luxuriously beside
Exists

Gouging
Orbs
Reduces
Diameters of
Individuality while
Ears drown in
Rivers of anxiety.

Death Stalks Me

Death stalks me
Lurking in silent shadows
Looming in doorways
Awaiting my demise

Death stalks my hearing
Sweet whispers
Begging through knives
Just one single cut

Death stalks my vision
Haunting my driving
Leering through others
Just one wrong turn

Death stalks my dreams
An assassin of vengeance
Swords plunged in my heart
Hoping I'll never awaken

Death never leaves me
I'm chained to his side
Depression and anxiety
Cause me to fall in his arms

Death's calling card
Bi-Polar disorder
Scars no one sees
Open wounds which never heal

To fight Death
Oh, so hard
And see six feet under
Yet again clawing out

One day
I'll not fight Death
The knife, car or dreams
One will take me to him

For I fear
I cannot fight forever
This dark laden foe
Cloaked in shadow beside me

So come,
come and take me
That I might breathe my last
And no more worries plague me

Finally,
I might smile upon Heaven or Hell
Come sweet Death
that we may dance upon my sorrows

No Hope for Seedlings

Somewhere in this dismal decay
A garden once was green and new
Small sprouts of every nature
Spread their leaflets to the sky

Now the gardener has gone
Weeds it then overrun
Sun baked the plot of earth
Then plants withered to none

How lonely this place must be
Lost without its caretaker
Ground now to dust
Beneath the crossing of feet

Seeds beneath the surface
Longingly cry out
Feed us, water us, please
Just a small chance for us

But there is no chance left
No hope for lost seeds
As skyscrapers are soon built
And the future trudges upon them

No Escape Plan

Drowning in darkness
Fear and despair
Black curling mist
In rooms of my mind

Deepening depression rises
Knives sweetly call
Watery depths croon
All tell me to come

Light has fled this place
No morning, day or dusk
Only blackest midnight
Now reigns here

No moon lights a path
Nor torch a hall
Death walks boldly
No escape plan

Migraine Pain

The Pain comes slowly
Like daggers placed by inches
First one, then two, then three
Into the spine, they're thrust

Daggers slowly twisted, each

Pain does not stop there
Three others make themselves known
One at the base of the neck
One to each shoulder blade

Each twisting slowly to torture me

How long have I lived this way?
How long has this pain been here?
I've lost count of so many years.
Twisting in torturous ruin

I've forgotten what it's like to be free

Now the shock to my head begins
Spikes suddenly pounded in
All thoughts flee from the pain
As another spike is driven through

Lights sparkle like flames before my eyes

I can do nothing but run and hide
Darkness is my only surcease
And rest to make the pain subside
No interruptions will do, then I'll be fine

Until a next migraine comes again.

Paris Torn & Loved

Sadness and hearts break,
As shots are fired,
Hostages taken,
Bombs blew,
People die.

Many left in streets,
Alleyways are full.
Distraught and shocked
Wander in vain.
Borders are closed.

Paris takes heed.

The call goes out wide,
On Facebook and Twitter,
Come one, come all.
Our homes we open,
Rest your weary heads.

Disorder & Solace

Bi-Polar Disorder
And
Insomnia
With nightmares
Have clashed.

Death
Has taken holiday
In my home and
Conversation
Has waxed.

Tears
Start flowing,
No reason given,
Emotions
Are mixed.

Moon passes
Slowly
Keeping time
With my
Sleepless TV fix.

No way to know
When sun will come
Until through
My window
Day finally breaks.

This poem
My only solace
From black deeds
When anxiety
Wreaks havoc.

The Knife Begs Release

The knife begs
It pleads
To be held
Plunged
Into flesh
Released

The knife begs
To feel
So quickly
Blood
Rush forward
Flowing

The knife begs
To hear
An even beat
A heart
Free of bonds
So foul

The knife begs
To see
All still
Quiet
Nothing moves
Released

Destruction Earth

I glance at
Tides of machinery
Walking over wild,
Losing expanses
Of nature.

My sight exploited
As men make glass
And iron rails dig deep,
Just as stone paths
Rot the land.

Steel wheel cogs
Churn water mills,
Water wells, oil wells -
Both on land and sea.
Black tears cover all.

I know not
Which struggle
Will cover
A broken heart
And a broken Earth.

Tired and Tormented

I am tired and tormented
Sailing a becalmed sea
Canvas has not moved
So many years past.

Provisions have long since run dry.

No waves have stirred
This tempting, silent sea
As the burning sun
Pounds down upon me.

Mirages form land beyond my reach.

I cannot live upon a ship
Where canvas is not stirred
By gusty summer winds
With clouds hot upon their heels.

Shade a vacant memory to weary eyes.

Can I live upon this ship?
Where even stars
Laugh at my lonely plight,
A mighty standoff with the sea.

On his throne, Neptune mocks me.

I seek to end this silent torment,
Angry sharp steel of sword,
Salty, sweet depth of sea.
Surely one will sweep me away.

Breath has been stolen from me.

Under a Blood Moon

Under a Blood Moon
Sharp edges hold promise
Of quiet release
As scarlet rivers flow

Darkness begins to speak
In soft, dulcet tones
While shadows whisper
A quiet, silent hope
Of six feet deep

Dawn sees slow ripples
Of blood rising on horizons
And thick, inky fog rises
To reveal a grave scene
Where Angels weep silent tears
For souls long past their rest

And Now…

I shall lay my weary head
Among these lost friends
To roam the bloody skies
As the Blood Moon rises

Death Whispers

Drain me dry
I've nothing left
Exhaustion speaks volumes

Though tears still come
Emotions are vague
And death whispers tomorrow

Knives, scissors, anything sharp
Shout my coming demise
All still sing so sweetly

Yet here I sit, ignoring the call
Wishing for relief so simple
From those who blindly grasp

For now, I am worn by claws
Men vicious and cruel by nature
Become the blades calling for me

I've little hope for escape
They fast fall upon me
Leaving little but for vultures

In the End

Somewhere inside this heart of mine
My soul aches to fly free
Soaring above the trees
Church bells toll the ending of time
Age turns a harsh master
Takes what youth gave faster
Soon I'll find Death is far more kind

"There can be no keener revelation of a society's soul than the way in which it treats its children." - Nelson Mandela

Society's Soul

Nelson Mandela
Voiced it true
Our treatment of children
Will reveal
A Society's Soul

In many years past
Love was our key
Living the Golden Rule
Do unto others
Give love unconditionally

We have strayed far
From the original path
The Golden Rule lays tarnished
Now we are left alone
With faces of our children
Missing on milk cartons

They are starved and abused
Glaring from televisions
Forced into workhouses
Making pittance for families
Thrown to societies wolves

We've turned away
Our blind eyes cannot see
The horrors we've made
The homes for our children
The place in our world

A mockery of ourselves
Hoping for the best
Getting the worst
In the end
Revealing the soul
Of our society

Lingering Death

My soul is broken
Cared for no longer
By those once loved
Shattered to pieces
On the floor

Silent ache
Of horrid memory
Soulmate so dear
Keeps death
Knocking at my door

Silent tears
Run down my cheek
Unbidden and unwelcome
Inviting death
Into my home

Sharp edges
Surrounding me
Whispering in my ears
Ask death
To take me away

Thinnest slice
On alabaster skin
Brings death closer
Task complete
He walks out my door

Tinnitus Hell

A wheeze, a hum
a tinny tweet,
a murmur in my mind.
Tinnitus holds me firmly
in its grasp.

www.ingramcontent.com/pod-product-compliance
Lightning Source LLC
LaVergne TN
LVHW020444080526
838202LV00055B/5335